Bronc Riding

Josepha Sherman

Heinemann Library
Chicago, Illinois

Designed by Lisa Buckley
Printed in Hong Kong

04 03 02 01 00
10 9 8 7 6 5 4 3 2 1

Library of Congress Cataloging-in-Publication Data
Sherman, Josepha.
    Bronc riding / Josepha Sherman.
       p. cm. – (Rodeo)
    Includes bibliographical references and index (p.)
    Summary: Explores the origins and development of bronc riding as a rodeo event, discussing the rules, the training, the judging, and the animal and human stars.
    ISBN 1-57572-504-5 (library binding)
    1. Bronc riding—Juvenile literature. [1. Bronc riding. 2. Rodeos.] I. Title.
GV1834.45.B75 S54 2000
791.8'4—dc21
                                                              99-054146

Acknowledgments
The author and publishers are grateful to the following for permission to reproduce copyright material: Dudley Barker, pp. 4, 21; Ben Klaffke, pp. 5, 8, 15, 16, 19; Steve Bly, pp. 6, 14, 17, 18, 22, 23; Corbis-Bettmann, pp. 6, 13; William A. Allard/National Geographic, pp. 9, 11; Chris Martin/Photo 20-20, p. 10; North Wind Picture Archives, p. 12; Dan Hubbell, p. 20; Jeff Greenberg/Photo Edit, p. 24; Corbis-Bettmann/UPI, p. 25; Jane Shaffer/Photo Edit, p. 26; Frank Siteman/Photo Edit, p. 27.

Cover photograph: Chris Martin/Photo 20-20

Special thanks to Dan Sullivan of the Calgary Stampede for his comments in the preparation of this book.

Every effort has been made to contact copyright holders of any material reproduced in this book. Any omissions will be rectified in subsequent printings if notice is given to the publisher.

Some words are shown in bold, **like this.**
You can find out what they mean by looking in the glossary.

Contents

Cowboy Versus Horse

The rodeo audience eagerly watches from the crowded grandstand as a horse is herded into a narrow **chute**. Cowboys sitting on the high rails of the chute are warily saddling the horse, who is tossing his head so wildly that the audience sees his mane waving. A cowboy eases himself down onto the horse.

A **bronc** rears in the chute. Cowboys rush to stop him and help the rider.

The bronco has won this round!

The gate to the chute flies open and out charges the horse. It starts bucking and spinning right away, clearly wanting the cowboy off its back. The cowboy hangs on with one hand. He spurs the horse all the while, although the audience knows that the spurring action makes a good show and makes it harder for the rider to stay on the horse. As for the horse, the spurs are too **blunt** to hurt.

Six seconds pass—seven—eight! A buzzer sounds. The cowboy has stayed on the full time! Now a **pickup man** brings his horse next to the bucking horse and helps the cowboy off. But the bucking horse is sure *he* has won! To the rodeo crowd's laughter, the horse races around the arena once, with its tail high in the air.

This is one small part of the story of cowboy and horse, a story that began a century ago.

Ranch Beginnings

In the 1800s, North American ranches were enormous. A man on horseback could ride a whole day without reaching a fence. In fact, during the nineteenth century, the King Ranch in Texas was larger than the state of Rhode Island.

Nowadays, cowboys speed along in trucks or helicopters. But in the 1800s, there were no modern forms of transportation. There was only the horse.

Horses were easy to find. Herds of mustangs, the wild horses, wandered the West. While some ranch horses were imported from the East, others were captured from the wild herds.

This is a roundup of ranch horses, going back to work after a summer off.

Bronc riding has been a popular event since the earliest days of rodeo.

The cowboy didn't have time for slow methods of training. Instead, he would quickly **break** a wild horse. After the horse was saddled and bridled, which often took several men to accomplish, the cowboy climbed onto its back, and the battle began. The cowboy would try to stay on until the horse stopped trying to throw him off.

These battles between man and horse entertained the other cowboys. Cowboys competed to see who could ride the wildest horse. Other people came to watch these contests, and from these working roots came the rodeo event of **bronc** riding.

The Bronc

This bronco isn't afraid of the cowboy, it just doesn't want him on its back.

A rodeo horse that bucks is called a **bronc** or a bronco. In the early days, broncs were wild horses. They didn't know what a rodeo was, or that no one was going to hurt them. A frightened horse who doesn't know what to expect is unpredictable. It might not buck at all. Or the horse might be so frightened that it flips, throwing itself over backwards. Today, the best rodeo bronc is a professional. It is as familiar with rodeos as a cowboy.

Two of the many ranches specializing in the breeding of bucking broncs are Kesler Rodeo of Montana and Alberta, Canada, and the Max Burch ranch in Wyoming. In fact, these ranches have been so successful that some rodeos have had four or five generations of horses from the same bronc family.

There are no rules about the type of horse a bronc must be. Some broncs might be **quarter horses** or **Thoroughbreds**. Some even are **draft horses** from farms. Most are **grade** horses of no known breed.

A good bucking bronc can leap and twist about like a cat, swapping ends, or turning around, in midair. A bronc can't be taught to buck. It has to be born with the will to buck and the skill to buck well.

Bucking horses aren't mean, though. A bronc usually doesn't want to hurt the cowboy trying to ride it. It will do its best not to step on a fallen rider to protect itself as well as the rider. Nor will a bronc attack a cowboy once he's on the ground.

Now that the cowboy is off its back, the bronc will settle down.

Why Do Horses Buck?

Even a tame horse has all the **instincts** of its wild cousins. All horses have a fear of **predators**, such as mountain lions, that might try to kill and eat it. A tame horse knows that a human rider isn't dangerous, but a wild horse doesn't know anything about humans. A cowboy might be a predator, too. Since predators attack horses by jumping on their backs, a wild horse will buck any time something lands on its back.

A horse's best defense is to run from danger.

Flank strap

Eight seconds on a bucking bronco can seem like hours!

Rodeo horses aren't wild. They're familiar with humans. So why do rodeo horses buck? All horses, even **foals**, will buck if their **flanks** are touched. So each **bronc** wears a **flank strap**, which is fleece-lined so it doesn't hurt the horse. The flank strap is never fastened tightly. It is there just to encourage the horse to buck.

Good broncs buck even without this strap. They simply do not want to be ridden. The truly professional bronc even stops bucking once it hears the ride-ending eight-second buzzer.

Early Rodeo

In the early days of official rodeos, **bronc** riding was one of the major events. Soon bronc riding was split into two categories, saddle bronc riding and bareback bronc riding.

Saddle bronc riding is based on the cowboy's ranch work of horse-breaking. Bareback bronc riding, as its name suggests, doesn't use a saddle and was created for the sport of rodeo. It was an event unknown to early working cowboys. Since the mid-1950s, it's been a required event at official rodeos.

In the early days of rodeo, cowboys had to get on the bronc without using a **chute.**

BRONCO BUSTERS SADDLING.

If a horse got spooked during ranch work, it could react like a bucking bronco.

In the early days of official rodeo, there weren't any chutes to hold a horse or bull steady until the event began. Chutes allow an animal to be quietly saddled. They also allow a cowboy to ease himself gently down onto the animal's back.

But with no chutes, a bronc had to be saddled and bridled in the arena. The bronc usually was scared and angry, so saddling and bridling would be a rodeo event in itself! Then as other cowboys hung onto the horse to keep it from running off or rearing up onto its hind legs, the rider climbed onto its back. Sometimes the cowboy didn't get very far if the horse broke loose or tossed him off before he even got into the saddle.

Gear

Bronc riding, like other rodeo sports, has specific rules about what can and cannot be used by the cowboy. Both saddle bronc riding and bareback bronc riding have the same rule about spurs. Spurs must be **blunt** so they can't hurt a horse. And both types of bronc wear **flank straps** that loosen as the horse bucks.

A saddle bronc doesn't wear a **bridle and bit**. That would make the horse too easy to control. Instead, all the bronc has on its head is a **halter**. A soft, woven bronc rein about six feet (two meters) long is attached to the halter. The bronc rein is all a saddle bronc rider may grab.

The saddle bronc's saddle is lined with fleece so that it won't hurt the horse's back. The **cinches**, which are the straps that fasten a saddle onto a horse, are made of soft **mohair** for the same reason.

Halter

Fleece-lined saddle

The bareback bronc doesn't wear a bridle or a halter. It doesn't wear a saddle, either. Instead, a thick leather pad, called the **rigging**, is cinched around the bronc's middle. At the front of this pad is a leather handhold. The handhold is all a bareback rider may grab.

Rigging and hand hold

Flank strap

The Rules:
Saddle Bronc Riding

A saddle bronc and rider charge out of the chute.

A saddle **bronc** is saddled in the **chute**. This makes saddling easier for the horse and the men. A saddle is gently lowered onto the bronc's back. Next, the dangling **cinches** are caught with a long-handled hook and raised to where they can be buckled. Then the **flank strap** is put in place.

The cowboy gently lowers himself into the saddle and takes a firm grip on the **bronc rein** with one hand. The chute gate opens. The bronc leaps out. The battle begins!

As the horse's front feet hit the ground, the cowboy's spurs must be in place up over the bronc's shoulders, or he will be disqualified. The cowboy will also be disqualified if he loses a stirrup, or if he lets his free hand touch anything but air.

He must find the right rhythm if he's going to stay in the saddle for the full eight seconds. The spurs, of course, are too dull to even annoy the bronc, but the action makes it more difficult to stay on board. Getting the timing wrong means a short flight off the horse and a hard landing into the arena dirt.

The cowboy spurs forward when the bronc kicks and moves back when the bronc jumps.

The Rules:
Bareback Bronc Riding

When the bronc bucks, the rider pulls up his knees.

As in saddle **bronc** riding, the bareback bronc is led into the **chute.** The **rigging** and **flank strap** are gently fastened. The cowboy carefully lowers himself onto the rigging's pad and takes a firm grip of the handhold. The chute is opened, and the bronc jumps out. Another battle begins!

The cowboy must **mark out** his horse. This means he has his feet above the bronc's shoulders right from the start. His feet must be there until the bronc's front feet hit the ground on the first leap out of the chute. If he's not in the right position, the cowboy is disqualified. Like the saddle bronc rider, he can't touch anything with his free hand.

This isn't an event for anyone who hasn't built up strength. Bareback bronc riding needs a strong arm, even more so than saddle bronc riding. All the power of the horse puts stress on the hand clinging to the stiff handhold. The cowboy is allowed to wear protective gloves, but that doesn't lessen the need for strength. The cowboy needs a good sense of balance, too. Once he loses balance and is thrown back from the handhold, he's sure to be bucked off.

A bareback bronc rider needs a strong arm!

Judging the Ride

It isn't enough for a cowboy to just stay in the saddle of the saddle **bronc** or on the back of the bareback bronc. He must stay there for eight seconds. This can seem like forever to a cowboy who's being jarred from head to toe by a jumping, bucking horse.

It's also not enough for a cowboy to just stay aboard for eight seconds. The two judges watching him will award as many as fifty points for his form and control. They want to know that it's the cowboy, not the bronc, who is in charge. But the judges can award up to fifty points for the bronc's performance as well.

A horse that is considered difficult to ride adds points to a cowboy's score.

20

Two rodeo judges size up an animal contestant.

The judges also decide whether a ride was fair. Every now and then, when the **chute** opens, the bronc merely stands there as though it were thinking things over. Sometimes the bronc refuses to leave the chute or decides to gallop about the arena instead of bucking. Sometimes the horse may slip and fall. In all of those cases in which the cowboy wasn't at fault, the judges allow the cowboy to have another ride.

Learning the Sport

A person can't just jump onto the back of a **bronc** and hope to stay on board. Staying on is a skill to be learned. Some cowboys learned their bronc riding skills on the ranch where they grew up. Ranch children growing up around horses often learn to ride as soon as they can sit in a saddle. They also learn not to be afraid of getting bucked off.

Other cowboys might start a bronc riding career when they are boys by entering rodeo events for children. Events such as sheep riding, in which the rider is usually five or six years old, give a child a taste of a bucking animal sport. Sheep riding, though, usually ends with the sheep running off and the child sitting on the ground.

A sheep rider gets his first taste of rodeo competition.

Still another way for a cowboy to learn bronc riding is to attend a bronc riding school. These schools usually last about three days and include classroom lessons as well as riding experiences. An advantage of attending a school is that a student has the chance to learn from a rodeo professional. A cowboy-in-training also has the chance to practice and perfect his skills on horses that aren't quite as tough as rodeo broncs.

Aside from just staying on the horse, a skilled bronc rider has to learn not to touch any part of his gear or his horse during the ride.

Bronc Riding Stars

Casey Tibbs

Casey Tibbs was one of the most famous professional rodeo cowboys. He is best known for winning six saddle **bronc** riding titles between 1949 and 1959. He also won a bareback bronc title and two all-around titles as well. A statue of Tibbs aboard the bucking horse, Necktie, stands outside the ProRodeo Hall of Fame in Colorado Springs, Colorado.

Marvin Garrett

Marvin Garrett won the title of World Champion Bareback Rider four times. In 1995, he also set a record for the most money won in one year by a bareback bronc rider— $156,733.

Tad Lucas

Dan Mortensen

In 1993, 1994, and 1995, and then again in 1997 and 1998, Dan Mortensen earned the title of World Champion Saddle Bronc Rider. He was also named the World Champion All-Around Cowboy in 1997.

Tad Lucas

Although women have not been allowed to ride bucking horses in North America since the 1930s, there have been female champions. One was Tad Lucas. From 1925 to 1933, she was All-Around Champion as well as Trick Riding Champion. In 1940, in Australia, she won the Australian Trophy for Best Buck Jumper, which means best bronc rider.

Retirement

Two old broncs enjoy their retirement.

There isn't a set retirement age for a cowboy or a **bronc**. A cowboy usually hangs up his spurs when he knows he's had enough. A bronc usually is retired from the rodeo when it loses interest in bucking. Since a bronc has to work only eight seconds a rodeo and is well-treated the whole time, a bronc might keep bucking into its teens.

What happens to a bronc after it is retired from the rodeo? The **geldings**, male horses who can't father **foals**, often go to live happily on a rancher's land. It's not unusual to see a little herd of retired bucking broncs living in peaceful old age together. The retired **mares**, the female broncs, often are sent to a breeding ranch to have foals. It's hoped that these foals will grow up to be bucking broncs, too. And they often do.

A bronco can pass on her good bucking qualities to her foal.

Associations and Rodeos

Associations:

American Junior Rodeo Association
6029 Loop 306 S.
San Angelo, Tex. 76905
(915) 2572

Canadian Professional Rodeo Association
223 2116 27th Avenue, NE
Calgary, Alberta, Canada T2E 7A6
(403)250-7440

Professional Rodeo Cowboys Association
101 ProRodeo Drive
Colorado Springs, CO 80919
(800)763-3648

Rodeos:

Bronc riding competitions can be seen at rodeos all over North America. Two of the biggest rodeos are:

Calgary Stampede
Calgary, Alberta, Canada
When: Early July
1-800-661-1767

Cheyenne Frontier Days
Cheyenne, Wyoming
When: Late July
1-800-227-6336

Past Champions

Saddle *Bronc* Riding

1998   Dan Mortensen, Manhattan, Mont.

1997   Dan Mortensen,
Manhattan, Mont.

1996   Billy Etbauer, Ree Heights, S.Dak.

1995   Dan Mortensen,
Manhattan, Mont.

1994   Dan Mortensen,
Manhattan, Mont.

1993   Dan Mortensen,
Manhattan, Mont.

1992   Billy Etbauer, Ree Heights, S.Dak.

1991   Robert Etbauer, Goodwell, Okla.

1990   Robert Etbauer, Ree Heights,
S.Dak.

1989   Clint Johnson, Spearfish, S.Dak.

1988   Clint Johnson, Spearfish, S.Dak.

1987   Clint Johnson, Spearfish, S.Dak.

1986   Bud Monroe, Valley Mills, Tex.

1985   Brad Gjermundson,
Marshall, N.Dak.

1984   Brad Gjermundson,
Marshall, N.Dak.

1983   Brad Gjermundson,
Marshall, N.Dak.

1982   Monty Henson, Mesquite, Tex.

1981   Brad Gjermundson,
Marshall, N.Dak.

1980   Clint Johnson, Spearfish, S.Dak.

Bareback Bronc Riding

1998   Mark Gomes, Hutchinson, Kans.

1997   Eric Mouton, Weatherford, Okla.

1996   Mark Garrett, Nisland, S.Dak.

1995   Marvin Garrett, Belle Fourche,
S.Dak.

1994   Marvin Garrett, Belle Fourche,
S.Dak.

1993   Deb Greenough, Red Lodge, Mont.

1992   Wayne Herman, Dickinson, N.Dak.

1991   Clint Corey, Kennewick, Wash.

1990   Chuck Logue, Decatur, Tex.

1989   Marvin Garrett, Belle Fourche,
S.Dak.

1988   Marvin Garrett, Belle Fourche,
S.Dak.

1987   Bruce Ford, Kersey, Colo.

1986   Lewis Feild, Elk Ridge, Utah

1985   Lewis Feild, Elk Ridge, Utah

1984   Larry Peabody, Three Forks, Mont.

1983   Bruce Ford, Kersey, Colo.

1982   Bruce Ford, Kersey, Colo.

1981   J.C. Trujillo, Steamboat Springs,
Colo.

1980   Bruce Ford, Kersey, Colo.

Glossary

blunt not sharp

break quick but rough way of taming a horse by getting on its back and riding until it stops bucking

bridle and bit head part of a horse's harness with a narrow strip of metal that fits into a horse's mouth

bronc, bronco bucking rodeo horse

bronc rein soft, woven strip of leather about six feet (two meters) long that is attached to some of the gear on a saddle bronc's head

chute holding pen that opens onto the arena

cinch buckled strap that holds a saddle or rigging in place

draft horse heavy, muscular farm horse

flank muscular side of a horse between the ribs and the hip

flank strap narrow, fleece-lined length of leather tied about a bronco's flank to encourage it to buck

foal baby horse

gelding male horse that cannot father a baby

grade horse horse with one purebred parent and one parent of no particular breed

halter rope or leather straps around a horse's head that help it be caught, led, or ridden

instinct built-in natural impulse

mane long fringe of hair on the back of a horse's neck

mare adult female horse

mark out bronc rider's starting position with his feet above the bronc's shoulders

mohair soft form of wool

pickup man   rider who brings his horse up against the bronc so the cowboy can dismount

predator   animal that hunts other animals for food

quarter horse   breed of horse known for quick starts and stops and great speed for a quarter of a mile

rigging   narrow leather pad, the strap around the horse's middle, and handhold used by a bareback bronc rider

Thoroughbred   breed of purebred horse generally used for racing

More Books to Read

Gabbert, Lisa. *An American Rodeo: Riding & Roping*. New York: Rosen Publishing Group, 1998.

Kirksmith, Tommie. *Ride Western Style: A Guide for Young Riders*. New York: Howell Books, 1991.

Rice, James. *Cowboy Rodeo*. Gretna, La.: Pelican Publishing Company, 1992.

Index

DATE DUE

1/8/03			